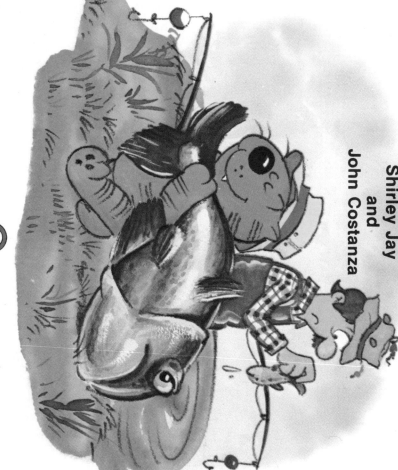

HEATHCLIFF®
The Fish Bandit

by
Shirley Jay
and
John Costanza

MARVEL BOOKS®

HEATHCLIFF® Copyright© 1983 McNaught Syndicate, Inc. All rights reserved. Published by Marvel Books, a division of Cadence Industries Corporation, 387 Park Avenue South, New York, NY 10016. ISBN 0-939766-52-3 Printed in Canada.

It's a beautiful morning! Heathcliff can't wait to begin the day. And the best way to begin is to plot for his breakfast.

Here comes the milk truck, racing around the corner. And Heathcliff is ready with a new milk-catching trap.

Will it work?

No, it won't! The milk truck isn't even stopping. It's rushing right past the Nutmeg's house.

The milkman has a big smile on his face and a fishing pole on the seat next to him. What can hungry Heathcliff do?

Heathcliff knows just how to get his well-deserved breakfast. Quickly, the clever cat dashes into the Nutmeg's house. He rummages around in the attic and finds just what he's looking for.

Now, it's time to put on a burst of speed. Heathcliff races the truck to the corner and holds up his sign.

Now he's got the milk truck just where he wants it!

With one glorious leap, Heathcliff is in milk-heaven! He purrs so loudly that he can't hear all the cars honking at the milk truck to get moving.

Ah, there's nothing better than breakfast — except maybe lunch or dinner.

Mean Spike and Muggsy love hearing all that noisy horn-honking. But they love the smell of milk better.

Spike is so fat, Muggsy has to push and heave to get him onto the truck.

One thing Heathcliff hates is unwanted guests.

Whew! All that exercise has made Heathcliff hungry for lunch. But there isn't going to be any fish today!

Heathcliff will have to catch his own fish. But first he needs fishing tackle. "STOP THAT RACKET!" everyone shouts.

But Heathcliff doesn't stop until he has all his gear — plus a raincoat.

He goes to his girlfriend Sonja's house and gets a bathtub to use as a boat. He's planning a combination fishing trip and romantic cruise. But how will he launch his trusty ship?

Iggy Nutmeg has an idea. It's a good thing he knows how to tie a knot! Slowly, but surely, he pulls the brave fishermen down the street. The whole block comes to see them off to the wild blue sea!

"You're on your own now!" Iggy shouts, launching the trusty tub. Heathcliff and Sonja are cozy as sardines in a can. It's a great day for a cruise.

It's time to start the outboard motor. What a trusty little ship they have. It floats like a dream over the salty sea.
And look at all those leaping fish, just begging to be caught!

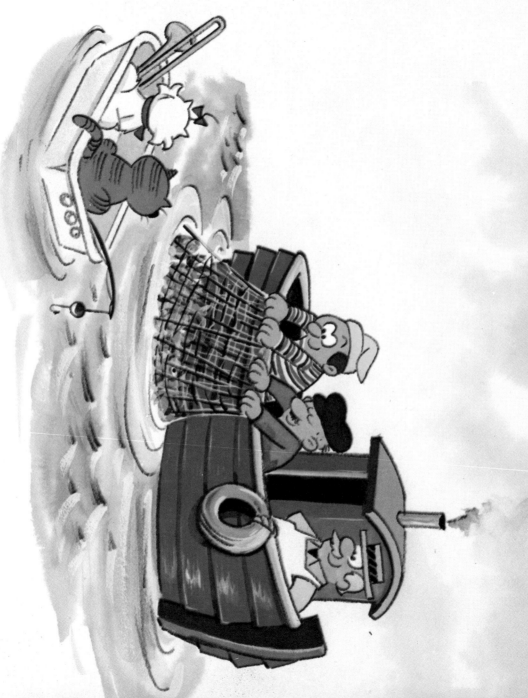

There's the big boat that belongs to the man from the fish-store. And look at all those hundreds of shiny fish he's just caught!

Sonja thinks Heathcliff's horn-playing is beautiful. The fishermen don't agree. And all those slippery fish slip back into the sea!

Fishing is really easy if you know how to do it! Soon, Heathcliff and Sonja are up to their whiskers in beautiful fish!

Better get those fish to shore!
Here come the fishermen, trying
to get even with the cat who
hijacked their fish!
    Heathcliff holds onto
Sonja as the waves
toss them around. But
one monster wave
tosses her overboard!

Sonja can't swim! But Heathcliff can think fast.
He hurls the fish out of the net and tosses
the net to Sonja.

How's Heathcliff going to get his tub back to shore? Then he sees a "strange toy."

Heathcliff takes a closer look at this "strange toy" Suddenly, it pulls Heathcliff overboard. But our hero simply ties the toy's strings to the bathtub.

"I've got a bite!" yells the milkman. "It's the biggest one all day. It's a whopper!" How he groans as he pulls and heaves his fish to shore.

Boy, is the milkman mad when he sees that his big catch is Heathcliff. That strange toy was the milkman's *float* attached to his fishing line. He's so angry he kicks his own bucket of fish over! Now he's HOPPING mad.

"I'll get you!" he yells.

But before he can, Heathcliff and Sonja hitch their tub to the milk truck. Life is beautiful once again. Fish taste terrific in the open air.

When the milk truck passes the Nutmeg home, Heathcliff cuts the cord loose from the bathtub. And now, the voyagers are home at last. The gallant Heathcliff hands his sweetheart a rose as a final parting memory of their day at sea.

"What a great catch!" Grandpa Nutmeg tells Heathcliff.

"There's enough fish to last for days," says Grandma.

"But where's my trombone?" Iggy wonders. "Ah, there it is!"

Iggy starts his trombone practice. But all that comes out is seaweed and shells!

"I'd rather hear the sound of the sea than that water-soaked trombone," yells Grandpa Nutmeg.

The smell of frying fish fills the house! Spike comes sniffing and snorting right in through the window. Heathcliff better protect his fish!

Armed with Iggy's baseball bat, Heathcliff chases the hungry Spike out of the house.

The milkman had so much bad luck fishing, he's decided to get back to work. "Ah," he thinks. "At least Heathcliff won't be here to bother me. He's still off in his tub."

"YIKES!" yells the milkman. "I can't believe it! I just can't get away from Heathcliff. He's everywhere."

But now everyone's happy — Heathcliff and the Nutmegs and the milkman — because all of them are having fish for supper!